This book belongs to

....

KU-032-569

NEE NAW

Leo, Bryce, Jackson, and Chase.
Bag of awesome! – D.Y.

To the BW Babies:
Ava, Isla, Isolde and Oli – P.B.

First published in 2018 by Scholastic New Zealand Limited
Private Bag 94407, Botany, Auckland 2163, New Zealand

Scholastic Australia Pty Limited
PO Box 579, Gosford, NSW 2250, Australia

Lyrics © Dean O'Brien (Mr Yipadee), 2018
Music © Dean O'Brien & The Song Store 2018
Illustrations © Paul Beavis, 2018

ISBN 978-1-77543-517-4

All rights reserved. No part of this publication may be reproduced or transmitted in
any form or by any means, electronic, mechanical or digital, including photocopying,
recording, storage in any information retrieval system, or otherwise, without prior
written permission of the publisher.

A catalogue record for this book is available from the National Library of New Zealand.

12 11 10 9 8 7 6 5 4 3 2 1   8 9/1   0 1 2 3 4 5/2

Illustrations created with hand-drawn line and Photoshop
Publishing team: Lynette Evans, Penny Scown and Sophia Broom
Designer: Vida & Luke Kelly Design
Typeset in Mr Anteater
Printed in China by RR Donnelley

Scholastic New Zealand's policy is to use papers that are renewable
and made efficiently from wood grown in responsibly managed forests,
so as to minimise its environmental footprint.

NEE NAW

and the Cowtastrophe

Words and Music by
Deano Yipadee

Illustrations by
Paul Beavis

SCHOLASTIC
AUCKLAND SYDNEY NEW YORK LONDON TORONTO
MEXICO CITY NEW DELHI HONG KONG

There was a dinky little fire truck,
napping away,
at the quiet fire station
one sunny day.

The big engines were on an important call.

They left him behind, saying:
"YOU'RE TOO SMALL!"

Then Granny phoned up.

"PLEASE HELP ME!

My poor cow, Ploppy,
is stuck up a tree!"

Nee Naw proudly sang,
and bounced out of bed.
He knew he could help,
no matter what they said.

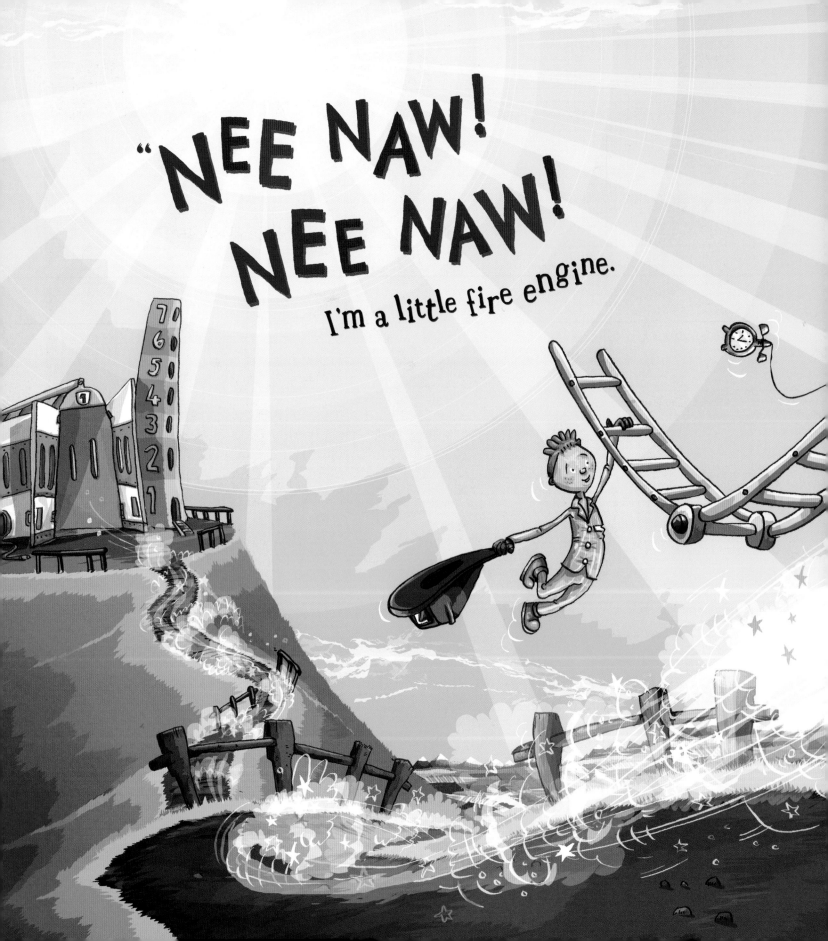

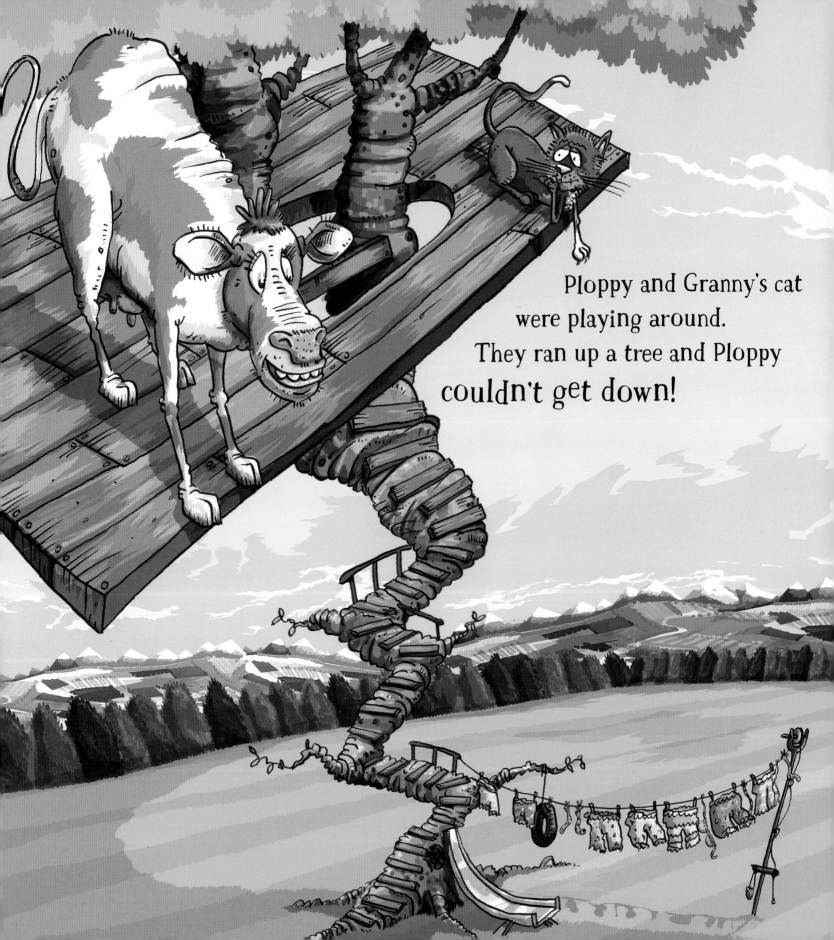

Ploppy and Granny's cat
were playing around.
They ran up a tree and Ploppy
couldn't get down!

A large, worried crowd
had gathered to see
the sight of a cow
that was stuck up a tree.

"If we stretch Granny's knickers
(they are very clean),
we could use those knickers
as a **trampoline!**"

But Granny's pants **ripped**,
and panic set in.

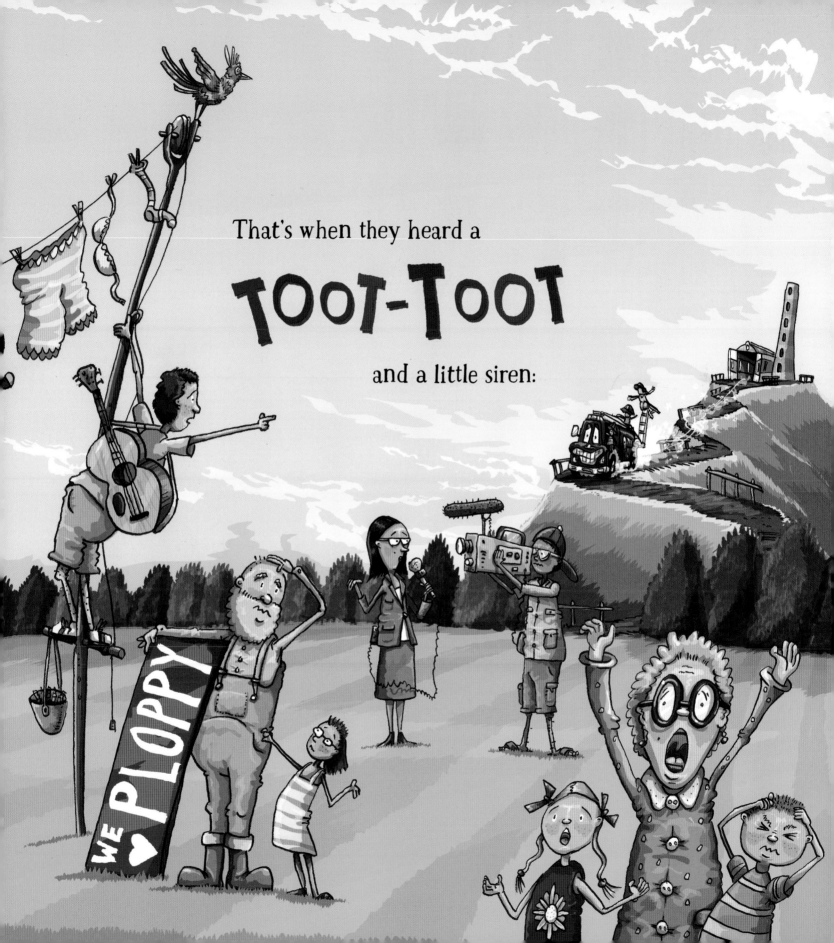

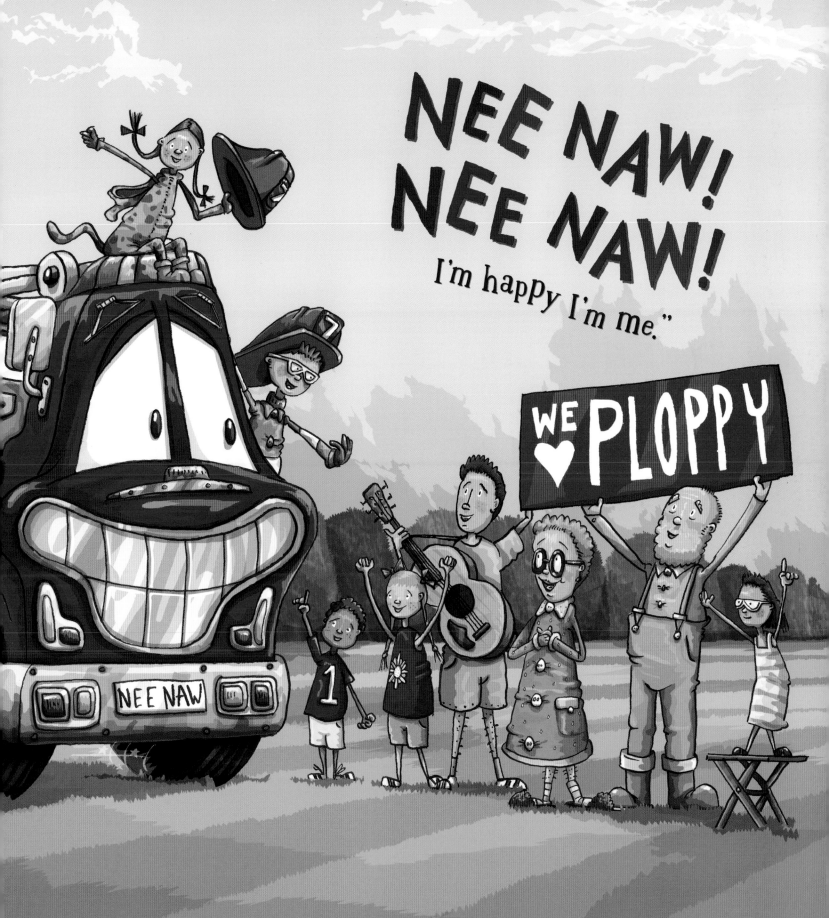

"Everyone, back! Stay calm,"
Nee Naw said.

WE ♥ PLOPPY

"I might slip," shrieked Ploppy,
"and donk my head!
I'm far too high,
and your ladder's too small!
Save me please, Nee Naw!
Or I might fall."

Nee Naw spoke calmly, "The answer lies with you.
You climbed the tree — you can climb down too.
If you start to wobble, if you trip, or yelp,
we'll be right here, and ready to help.

"Close your eyes, Ploppy, **breathe** with me. See yourself stepping down the tree ...

safe and steady, all the way to the ground."

The crowd was so still ... not a soul made a sound.

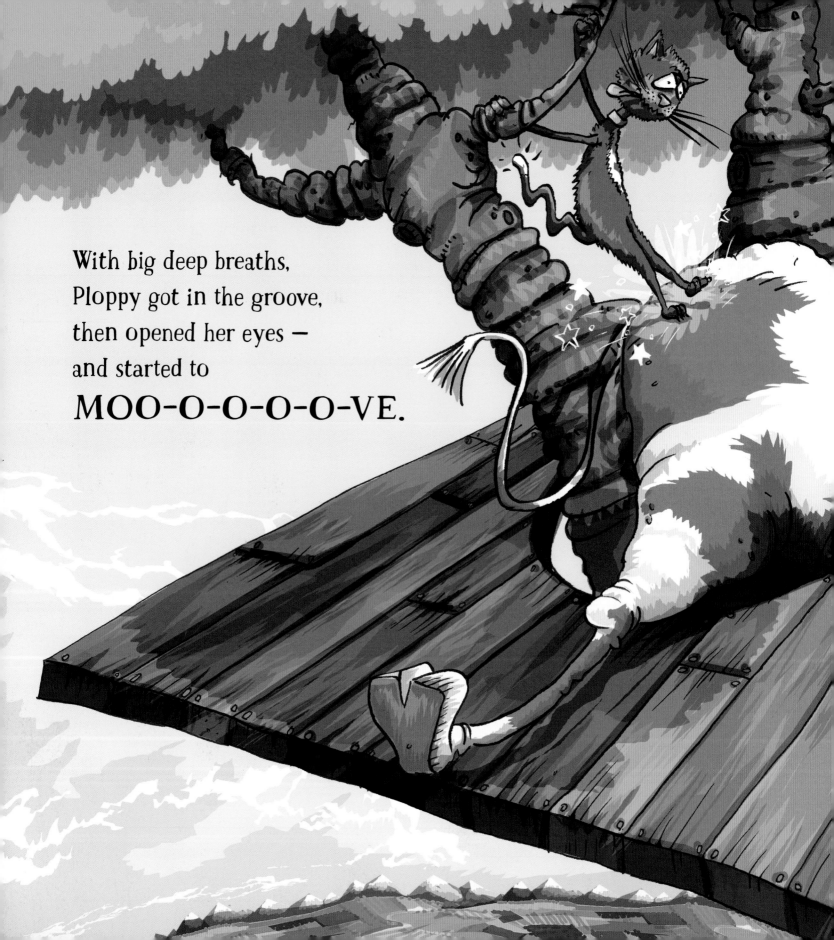

With big deep breaths,
Ploppy got in the groove,
then opened her eyes –
and started to
MOO-O-O-O-O-VE.

She said "I can do it,"
and climbed down the tree,
taking strong, steady steps:

one ...
two ...
three!

As she took the last step,
the crowd yelled:

"HOORAY"

because Ploppy had got herself down,
all the way.

WE ♥ PLOPPY

With excited cries from the cat,

"Me-e-e-o-o-ow!"

and big hugs for Nee Naw — from Ploppy the cow.

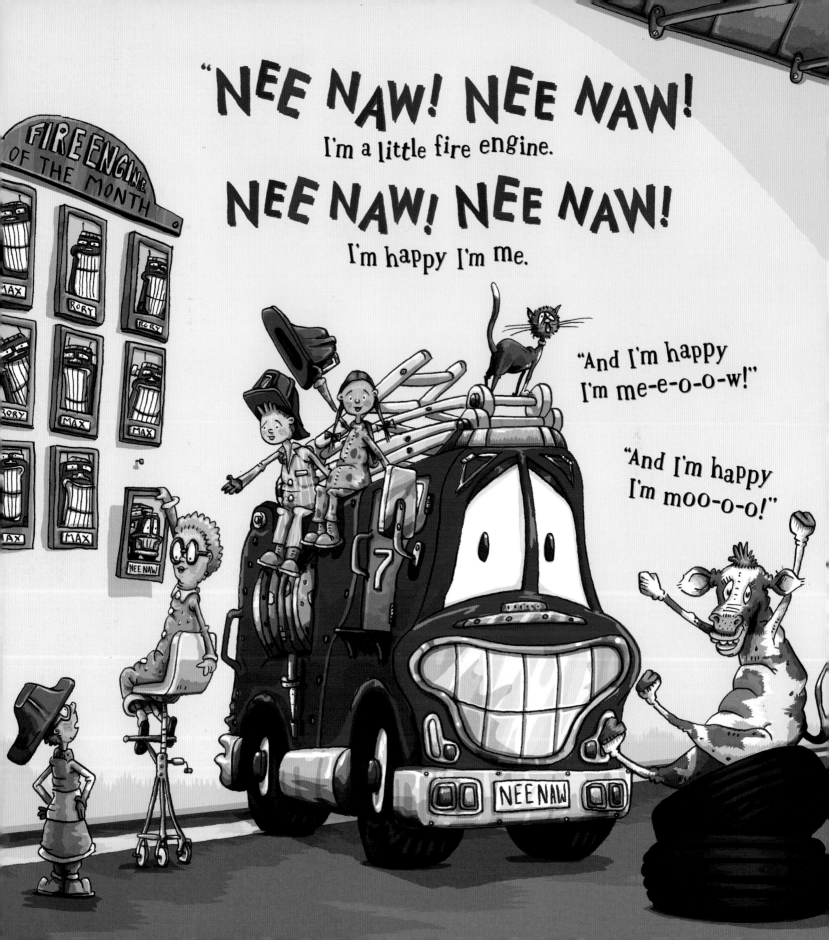